FANEUIL HALL

Faneuil Hall was built by a Boston merchant, Peter Faneuil, in 1742, then given by him to the city as a gift. The first floor was a central market, and the second was a town hall. So many important gatherings in protest of British policies took place at Faneuil Hall that the building has been called the "Cradle of Liberty." A golden grasshopper weather vane on top of Faneuil Hall is one of the most famous landmarks of Boston.

PAUL REVERE HOUSE

Paul Revere was one of the great patriots of the American Revolution. On the night of April 18, 1775, Revere learned that British soldiers were on their way from Boston to Lexington to arrest Samuel Adams and John Hancock and to Concord to destroy military supplies stored by the colonial militia. Revere rode through the countryside warning, "The Redcoats are coming!" He made it to Lexington, but was captured by British patrols on the road to Concord. Fortunately, another patriot who was with Revere was able to ride on to warn the militia at Concord. Paul Revere's House is the oldest building in downtown Boston.

OLD NORTH CHURCH

The Old North Church, built in 1723, is the oldest church building in Boston. Before Paul Revere set out on his historic ride to Lexington and Concord, he arranged with the sexton of the Old North Church to flash a signal to the patriots in Charleston that the British were on the way. One lantern would be hung in the church steeple if the British were coming by land; two lanterns would be hung if the British were coming by sea. The British went "by sea," that is, across the Charles River rather than by the longer, strictly land route, so two lanterns were hung in the steeple.

OLD SOUTH MEETING HOUSE

The Puritans referred to their house of worship as a "meeting house." The Old South Meeting House was built in 1729. In the years before the Revolution, it was often used for town meetings, especially if the crowd was too large to fit into Faneuil Hall. The largest such meeting took place on December 16, 1773, when 5,000 angry Bostonians met to protest British actions in connection with a tax on tea. That night, a group of patriots, many disguised as Native Americans, boarded British ships carrying tea and dumped the cargo into Boston Harbor. We call this event the Boston Tea Party.

OTHER SIGHTS ON THE FREEDOM TRAIL™

There are many other revolutionary era sights to see on the Freedom Trail™ — King's Chapel and King's Chapel Burying Ground, Benjamin Franklin's Statue, the Site of the First Public School in the United States, the Old Corner Bookstore, the Old State House, the Boston Massacre Site, Copp's Hill Burying Ground, and the Bunker Hill Monument.

Emily Breaks Free

Written by Linda Talley

Illustrated by Andra Chase

MarshMedia, Kansas City, Missouri

To Amber   *L.T.*

To Kirby Ann   *A.C.*

Special thanks to Karen Maree Thompson
and to the Freedom Trail™ Foundation.

Text © 2000 by Marsh Film Enterprises, Inc.

Illustrations © 2000 by Marsh Film Enterprises, Inc.

First Printing 2000

Second Printing 2004

Published by **MARSH**media

A Division of Marsh Film Enterprises, Inc.
P. O. Box 8082
Shawnee Mission, KS 66208

Library of Congress Cataloging-in-Publication Data
Talley, Linda.
    Emily breaks free / written by Linda Talley; illustrated by Andra Chase.
       p. cm.
    Summary: While on her daily walk, Emily goes along when Spike bullies a dog visiting from Georgia, until a more considerate dog named Emerson helps her realize that bullying is no fun.
    ISBN 1-55942-155-X
    [1. Dogs—Fiction. 2. Bullies—Fiction. 3. Boston (Mass.)—Fiction.]
I. Chase, Andra, ill. II. Title.
PZ7.T156355 Em 2000   00-031878
[E]—dc21

Book layout and typography by Cirrus Design

Printed in Hong Kong

Emily loved mornings. On with the leash, down the hallway, into the elevator. Once Emily and her mistress were out onto Beacon Street, they were only a few steps from Boston Common. Then the fun part. The frisbee. Every time it sailed through the air, Emily ran after it, caught it, and brought it back to her mistress. Again and again and again. Never too many times. This was a normal morning for Emily.

Today was definitely *not* a normal morning for Cotton. She had traveled all the way from Georgia to Boston the night before. Now she was trotting down an unfamiliar street beside her family. Cotton didn't like being a tourist and wasn't the teeniest bit interested in the American Revolution or Benjamin Franklin or Paul Revere or the Boston Tea Party.

Well, maybe the tea party had possibilities, but so far she hadn't been invited for tea at any of the places her family had visited. Instead she had been tied up outside like one of the ponies back on the farm.

"One more," called Emily's mistress. Emily ran with her eyes on the frisbee as it sailed overhead. But just as she arched her neck to make the catch, a gust caught the frisbee, carrying it over a hedge and out of sight.

Emily scurried through the hedge, then stopped.
"Oh, no," she gasped. "Spike!"

9

Emily's frisbee was clenched in the smiling muzzle of a large red dog. It was not a friendly smile.

"Please, Spike!" she implored. "Please give me back my frisbee." Spike shook his head no, still grinning. Then he made a run for the street.

"That does it," said Emily.

As she took off after Spike, she heard the fading sound of her mistress' voice. "Emily! Come back here!" But Emily kept right on going. She had to get her frisbee back.

Meanwhile, Cotton was sitting alone and unhappy outside a red brick building, her leash fastened to a signpost. She was trying to muster positive thoughts about the tea party when a red dog came running down the street, a frisbee in his muzzle and a small black dog at his heels.

When Spike saw Cotton, he stopped short and let the frisbee fall from his mouth. Emily watched in dismay as it clattered into the street and down a storm drain. Emily knew her frisbee was gone forever. She turned angrily toward Spike, but Spike was paying no attention to Emily or her frisbee now.

"Well," he snickered as he bent to read the letters embroidered on Cotton's dog collar. "Aren't you a good little doggie . . . COTTON." He laughed again. "What on earth kind of name is that?"

"Where I come from folks think it's a very fine name," said Cotton.

Emily wondered where Cotton came from and why she was here in Boston. She started to ask, but was interrupted by another howl of laughter from Spike. "Well, your name fits you! You're nothing more than a little ball of fuzz!"

Emily thought that was a mean thing to say, and she felt bad about the hurt look on Cotton's face, but Spike laughed so loud and Cotton looked so much like her funny name that Emily laughed too.

Just then Cotton's family came out of the red brick building and unfastened Cotton's leash from the signpost. In a moment Cotton was trotting down the sidewalk beside her family.

"Hey, Emily!" called Spike. "We don't want to miss out on this! Let's go too!" Emily ran after Spike. Even though he had cost Emily her frisbee, Spike had made her laugh. He was kind of fun, and Emily was glad that he wanted her to come along.

Cotton and her family followed a winding path around town, stopping occasionally to read a placard or admire a building. Emily and Spike trailed not far behind. Occasionally Cotton peered back at them with a worried expression.

At Richmond Street, Cotton and her family stopped in front of a very old wooden building. Cotton barked in excitement. Paul Revere's house! Maybe Mr. Revere was having the tea party! But Cotton's excitement didn't last long. Her chattering family trooped inside, leaving her with her leash fastened to a lamppost. Her only consolation was the little pile of dog biscuits left at her feet.

"Well, well, well," said Spike. "Look what the good little doggie has!" He crunched away on Cotton's dog biscuits. "And good little doggies know they are supposed to share with their friends," he said, picking up Cotton's last biscuit and dropping it under Emily's nose.

"Here, Em," he said with a wink, crumbs falling from his mouth.

Emily looked at Cotton's stricken face and then at Spike's expectant one. She gobbled the biscuit down, but it didn't taste as good as she had thought it would.

"I declare!" cried Cotton. "I do believe the dogs in this town are the meanest ol' dogs I have ever had the misfortune to encounter!"

Emily didn't really like being lumped in a group with Spike. She wanted to protest that she was usually a very nice dog, that she was just wanting to have fun, but that somehow things had gotten all confused today. She was thinking how to make things right when she realized that Spike was laughing again.

"You talk so funny!" he laughed. Spike was right. Cotton didn't talk anything like the dogs in Boston! Emily started to laugh too. "Where are you from anyway?" asked Spike. "Mars?"

"No, she's not from Mars," came another voice. "She's from the South."

Spike and Emily turned to stare at a bewhiskered dog with a friendly face, who was sauntering across the sidewalk toward them.

"Oh, great," said Spike with a sneer. "It's Emerson. Who invited you, anyway?"

"Well, I don't think you own this sidewalk, do you?" asked Emerson. Without waiting for an answer, Emerson turned to Cotton. "Where exactly are you from?"

Spike looked at Emily and rolled his eyes. "Mr. Nice Guy," he muttered.

"Yes," thought Emily, "this Emerson does seem like a nice guy."

"I'm from Georgia," said Cotton proudly. "My family lives on a farm and raises cotton, and that's why they named me Cotton. Yesterday we flew here in an airplane and in a few days we are going to sail in a sailboat all the way back to Savannah, Georgia. My family takes me with them everywhere they go."

Emily could not believe her ears. She had never known any dog who came from the South or had flown in an airplane or sailed all the way from Boston to Savannah, Georgia. If Emerson hadn't come along, she might never have found this out.

Emily's thoughts were interrupted by Spike.

"Your family takes you with them everywhere they go because they know you would get lost if you weren't tagging along behind them," he sneered. Then he ran for Cotton's leash and with a SNAP tore it from the lamppost.

"Come on, you guys!" Spike called. He gave a yank on Cotton's leash that left her sprawled on the sidewalk. "Let's have some fun! Let's see how the little fuzz ball does on her own!"

"I don't think that sounds like much fun at all," answered Emerson.

"We don't need you, Mr. Nice Guy," said Spike. "Come on, Emily!" he barked.

Emily looked at Emerson. He didn't move. Emily turned back to Spike, then called out defiantly, "Hey, you're not my boss! I don't want to go with you, and I'm not!" Emily liked the way her voice sounded when she said that.

Spike looked totally exasperated.

"And I think you better put down my leash right this minute, you big bully!" demanded Cotton.

Spike spit out Cotton's leash. "Well, aren't you guys a barrel of laughs," he muttered. Then he turned and loped off by himself down the block. He looked back over his shoulder one time, and then he was gone.

"Good riddance!" said Cotton. "Thank you, Emerson," she added. "I do believe you are the most considerate dog I have ever met." She hesitated for a moment, then looked at Emily out of the corner of her eye. "And an inspiration to us all, I'm sure."

They all three laughed as they plopped on the sidewalk together. Cotton told Emerson and Emily all about Georgia and airplanes and tea parties at home. Emily and Emerson told Cotton all about the Boston Tea Party and Redcoats and Paul Revere. They visited until it was time for Cotton and her family to be on their way and for Emily and Emerson to start back to their homes.

"Say," laughed Cotton as they said their goodbyes, "I guess we had our own revolution here today! We're free of Spike!"

"And free to be friends!" laughed Emily. That was the best part of all.

Dear Parents and Educators:

As children become socially active, they discover that occasional disagreements with friends, neighbors, and classmates are a fact of life. With time and experience, by trial and error, and guided by positive adult role models, children become increasingly skillful at resolving these everyday conflicts for themselves without the need for adult intervention.

But when conflicts include repetitive physical or verbal abuse of one child by another — and especially when there is an imbalance of power (physically, emotionally, or cognitively) between the abuser and the abused — we identify the situation as bullying. Bullying is a serious problem for youngsters and one that they need help understanding and countering.

The story of *Emily Breaks Free* looks at the dynamics of bullying and shows how this dynamic involves a larger cast of characters than just the bully and the target. Essential to the bully's sense of self-importance is the presence of an audience and support group, drawn from the many youngsters whose values are not clearly defined and who are susceptible to the sense of excitement and danger the bully offers to his cheering section. But this same group is also susceptible to the positive influence of those whose values are clearly defined, those who can always be relied on to respect the rights of others. Such an individual can inspire and influence the wavering majority to take a courageous stand against the bully.

Emily Breaks Free is a way to discuss bullying with young people in a deliberate manner. Here are some questions to help initiate discussion about the message of *Emily Breaks Free*.

- Which character in the story used bullying behavior?
- What kind of behaviors did this include?
- What do you think this character was thinking?
- How do you think he was feeling?
- Which character was being "picked on"?
- What do you think this character was thinking?
- How do you think she was feeling?
- What did Emily do when Spike was mean to Cotton?
- Could she have made a better choice?
- How do you think Emily was feeling when Spike looked to her for support?
- Who taught Emily to be courageous and kind?
- How do you think Emily was feeling at the end of the story?
- How do you think Spike was feeling at the end of the story?

Available from MarshMedia

These storybooks, each hardcover with dustjacket and full-color illustrations throughout, are available at bookstores, or you may order at www.marshmedia.com or by calling toll free: 1-800-821-3303.

Aloha Potter! Written by Linda Talley, illustrated by Andra Chase. 32 pages. ISBN 1-55942-200-9.

Amazing Mallika, written by Jami Parkison, illustrated by Itoko Maeno. 32 pages. ISBN 1-55942-087-1.

Bailey's Birthday, written by Elizabeth Happy, illustrated by Andra Chase. 32 pages. ISBN 1-55942-059-6.

Bastet, written by Linda Talley, illustrated by Itoko Maeno. 32 pages. ISBN 1-55942-161-4.

Bea's Own Good, written by Linda Talley, illustrated by Andra Chase. 32 pages. ISBN 1-55942-092-8.

Clarissa, written by Carol Talley, illustrated by Itoko Maeno. 32 pages. ISBN 1-55942-014-6.

Dream Catchers, written by Lisa Suhay, illustrated by Louis S. Glanzman. 40 pages. ISBN 1-55942-181-9.

Emily Breaks Free, written by Linda Talley, illustrated by Andra Chase. 32 pages. ISBN 1-55942-155-X.

Feathers at Las Flores, written by Linda Talley, illustrated by Andra Chase. 32 pages. ISBN 1-55942-162-2.

Following Isabella, written by Linda Talley, illustrated by Andra Chase. 32 pages. ISBN 1-55942-163-0.

Gumbo Goes Downtown, written by Carol Talley, illustrated by Itoko Maeno. 32 pages. ISBN 1-55942-042-1.

Hana's Year, written by Carol Talley, illustrated by Itoko Maeno. 32 pages. ISBN 1-55942-034-0.

Inger's Promise, written by Jami Parkison, illustrated by Andra Chase. 32 pages. ISBN 1-55942-080-4.

Jackson's Plan, written by Linda Talley, illustrated by Andra Chase. 32 pages. ISBN 1-55942-104-5.

Jomo and Mata, written by Alyssa Chase, illustrated by Andra Chase. 32 pages. ISBN 1-55942-051-0.

Kiki and the Cuckoo, written by Elizabeth Happy, illustrated by Andra Chase. 32 pages. ISBN 1-55942-038-3.

Kylie's Concert, written by Patty Sheehan, illustrated by Itoko Maeno. 32 pages. ISBN 1-55942-046-4.

Kylie's Song, written by Patty Sheehan, illustrated by Itoko Maeno. 32 pages. (Paper Posie, LLC) ISBN 0-911655-19-0.

Ludmila's Way, written by Linda Talley, illustrated by Andra Chase. 32 pages. ISBN 1-55942-190-8.

Minou, written by Mindy Bingham, illustrated by Itoko Maeno. 64 pages. (Paper Posie, LLC) ISBN 0-911655-36-0.

Molly's Magic, written by Penelope Colville Paine, illustrated by Itoko Maeno. 32 pages. ISBN 1-55942-068-5.

My Way Sally, written by Mindy Bingham and Penelope Paine, illustrated by Itoko Maeno. 48 pages. (Paper Posie, LLC) ISBN 0-911655-27-1.

Papa Piccolo, written by Carol Talley, illustrated by Itoko Maeno. 32 pages. ISBN 1-55942-028-6.

Pequeña the Burro, written by Jami Parkison, illustrated by Itoko Maeno. 32 pages. ISBN 1-55942-055-3.

Plato's Journey, written by Linda Talley, illustrated by Itoko Maeno. 32 pages. ISBN 1-55942-100-2.

Tessa on Her Own, written by Alyssa Chase, illustrated by Itoko Maeno. 32 pages. ISBN 1-55942-064-2.

Thank You, Meiling, written by Linda Talley, illustrated by Itoko Maeno, 32 pages. ISBN 1-55942-118-5.

Time for Horatio, written by Penelope Paine, illustrated by Itoko Maeno. 48 pages. (Paper Posie, LLC) ISBN 0-9707944-7-9.

Toad in Town, written by Linda Talley, illustrated by Itoko Maeno. 32 pages. ISBN 1-55942-165-7.

Tonia the Tree, written by Sandy Stryker, illustrated by Itoko Maeno. 32 pages. (Paper Posie, LLC) ISBN 0-911655-16-6.

Companion videos and activity guides, as well as multimedia kits for classroom use, are also available. MarshMedia has been publishing high-quality, award-winning learning materials for children since 1969. To order or to receive a free catalog, call 1-800-821-3303, or visit us at www.marshmedia.com.

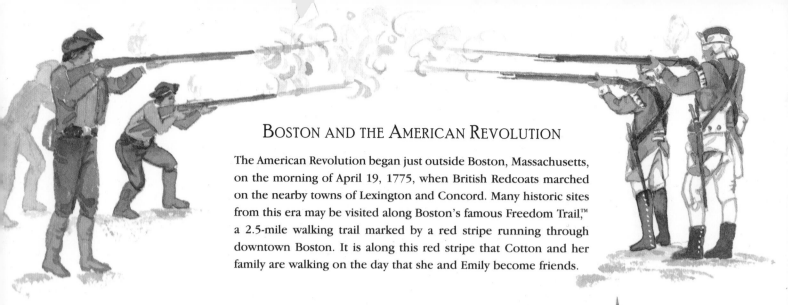

BOSTON AND THE AMERICAN REVOLUTION

The American Revolution began just outside Boston, Massachusetts, on the morning of April 19, 1775, when British Redcoats marched on the nearby towns of Lexington and Concord. Many historic sites from this era may be visited along Boston's famous Freedom Trail,™ a 2.5-mile walking trail marked by a red stripe running through downtown Boston. It is along this red stripe that Cotton and her family are walking on the day that she and Emily become friends.

THE STATE HOUSE

The cornerstone of the seat of the Massachusetts state government was laid in 1795 by the Revolutionary War patriots Samuel Adams and Paul Revere. The building was completed in 1798. The gold dome on the State House is fifty feet in diameter and thirty feet high. In the Hall of Representatives hangs the Sacred Cod, a five-foot-long wooden fish symbolizing the importance of the fishing industry to Massachusetts.

GRANARY BURYING GROUND

The Granary Burying Ground was founded in 1660. Among the 1600 graves are those of many patriots — Samuel Adams, Crispus Attuks, Peter Faneuil, John Hancock, and Paul Revere. This cemetery is called the Granary Burying Ground because a grain storage building was on the site before the cemetery was founded.

BOSTON COMMON

Most people begin their walk along the Freedom Trail™ at the Boston Common. In 1634, the land that is now the Boston Common was set aside as a public pasture, to be used in "common" by all the townspeople. Although cows and sheep grazed there as late as 1830, the Common was put to many other uses over the years. British troops drilled there before their march on Lexington and Concord in 1775. Thieves, Quakers, and women convicted of witchcraft were hung from the gallows there. The Common was the site for duels, band concerts, and public meetings. Today workers from nearby offices and shops eat lunch there in fine weather, strollers feed pigeons, and, in the winter, children skate on the frog pond.